MW00976923

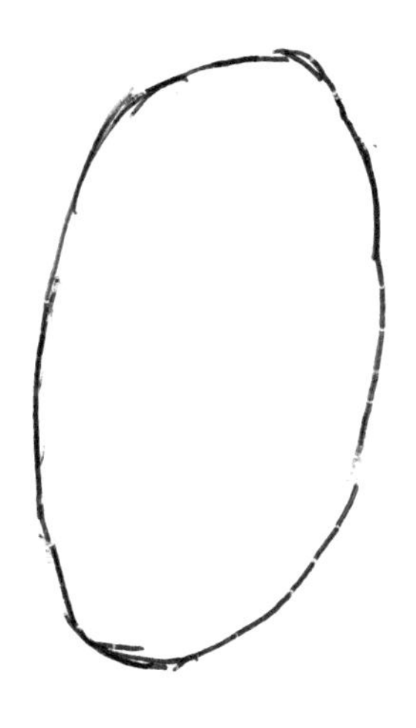

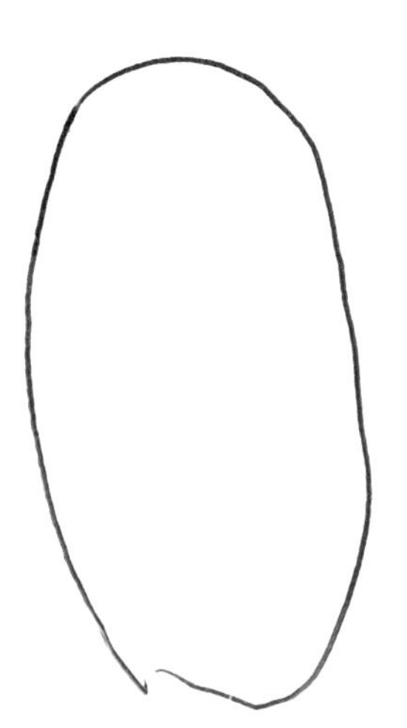

Stinky SHOES

Author: Debra J. Mines
Illustrator: Henry M. Blackmon III

Stinky Shoes

Illustrations Created by: Henry M. Blackmon III

iUniverse books may be ordered through booksellers or by contacting:

iUniverse
1663 Liberty Drive
Bloomington, IN 47403
www.iuniverse.com
1-800-Authors (1-800-288-4677)

ISBN: 978-1-5320-2499-3 (sc)
ISBN: 978-1-5320-2501-3 (hc)
ISBN: 978-1-5320-2500-6 (e)

Library of Congress Control Number: 2017908441

Printed in China

iUniverse rev. date: 08/24/2017

Afterword

The idea for Stinky Shoes was developed by the author, Debra J. Mines, when she presented her "magic box" to students in the DeKalb County School District in Atlanta, Georgia. Initially, the "magic box" was a decorated shoebox that held a pair of mysteriously, stinky shoes.

Eventually, this box transformed into a magic box with the story, "Stinky Shoes," becoming the focus and, ultimately, the title of Debra J. Mines' book, Stinky Shoes. The birth of this book, Stinky Shoes, was inevitable, because the author's students wanted to hear this story read over and over and over again! In response to their enthusiasm for Stinky Shoes, it was selected to be the first book for publication by the author, Debra J. Mines.

Special Thanks

Special thanks is given to my daughter, Hermalena Powell, for her compliments and critical analysis; to my son-in-law, Matthew Powell, and grandchildren: Alaina and Alan, for listening to my stories with attentive ears; to my son, Clifford Mines, and daughter-in-law, Ligelou Ponce Mines, for providing encouraging words as I set up a timeline for the completion of Stinky Shoes; and to my cousins: Betty Williams, Stacie Veal and her children, for patiently appreciating the crude illustrations that I drew for the first draft of Stinky Shoes.

Author's Dedication

I dedicate this book to my lovely mother, Mrs. Charlene N. Seymour Whittenburg, for being an avid writer and motivating me to write, as well.

Illustrator's Dedication

I, Henry Blackmon III, dedicate this book to my parents, Henry and Mary Blackmon, for their constant support throughout the years, and to my wife, Carmella Blackmon, who picked up the ball and helped lift me to greater heights as an artist, and most importantly, a man. I also would like to dedicate this book to my young sons, Henry IV and Cameron, who inspired me beyond measure throughout the entire process. It is my hope that my sons are inspired to pursue their dreams like Dad has in creating the illustrations for this adventurous tale of Stinky Shoes.

Phew-oo-oo-oo-wee!

Do you have a pair of Stinky Shoes?

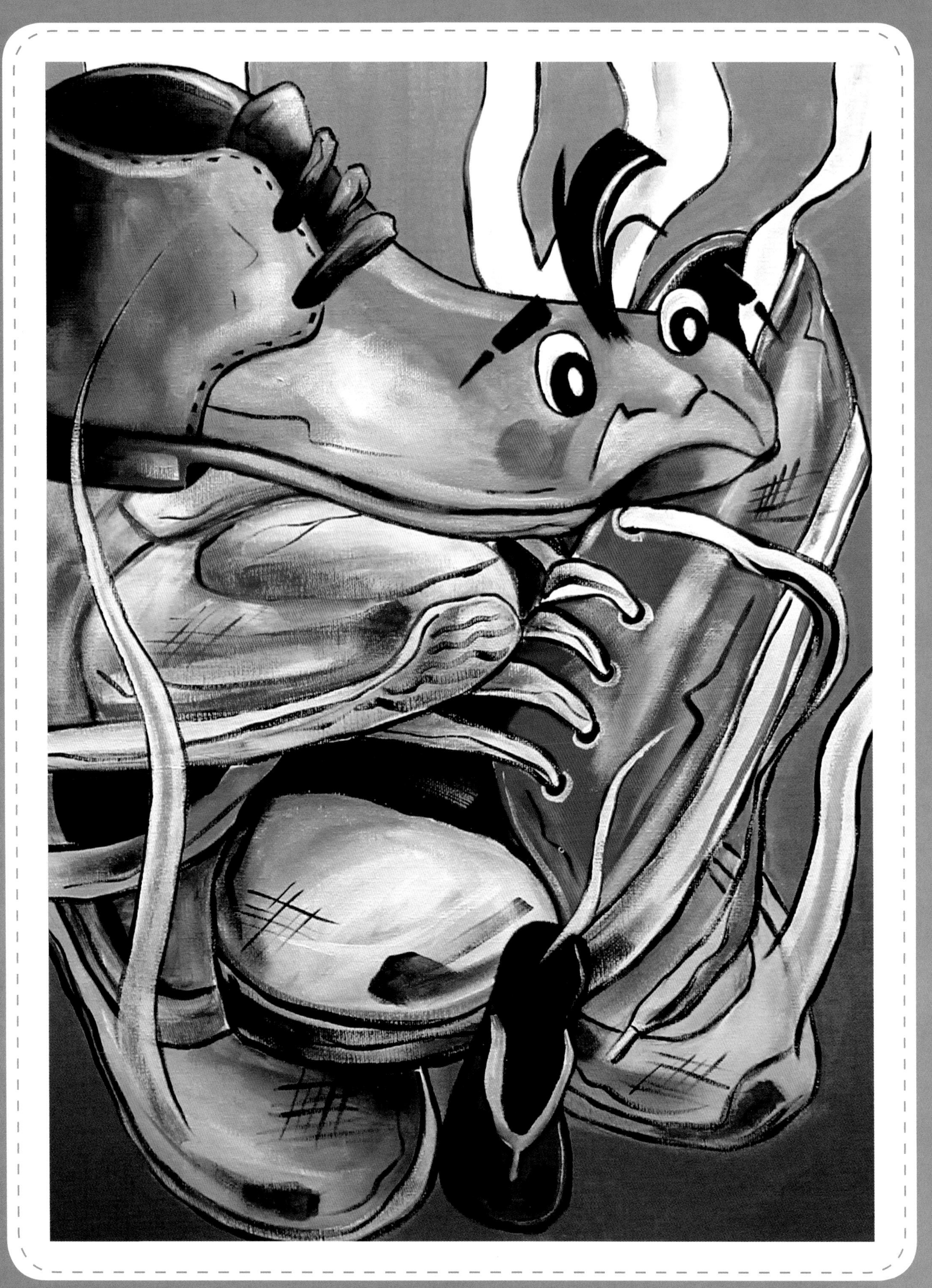

That's me ....

But I wasn't always stinky. There was a time, not long ago, when I lived on a clean shelf in a clean shoe store.

I smelled good and I looked good, too.

But I wasn't happy there.

I was tired of sitting on that boring shelf.

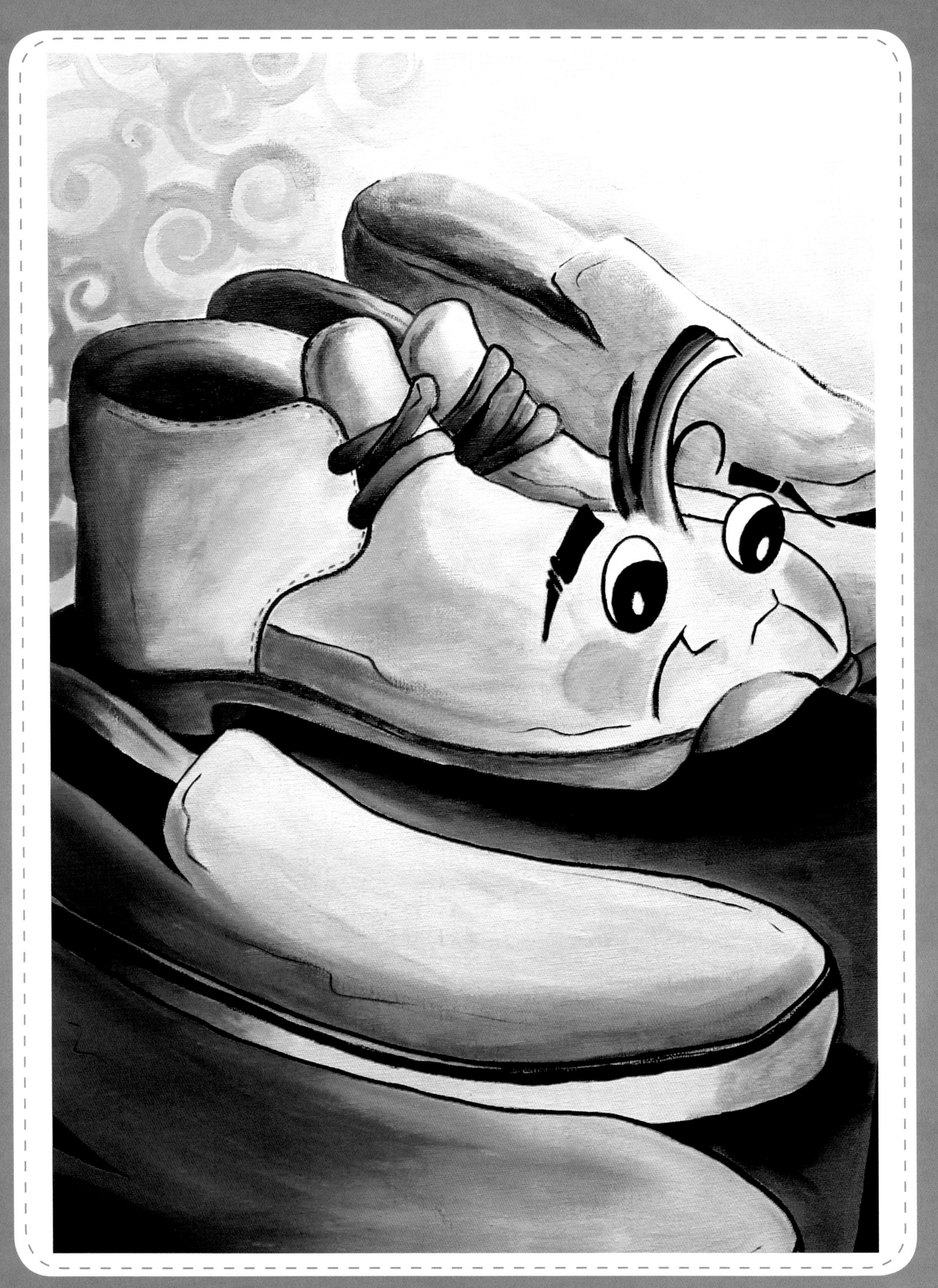

Instead, I wished that I could jump into a racecar and speed out of the shoe store....

"Br-r-r-r-r-r-um-m-m-m-m-m-m-m-m-m-m-m-m-m-m-m-m-m-m-m," I thought. "Br-r-r-r-r-r-r-r-r-r-r-r-rum-rum-m-m-m-m-m-m-m-m-m-m-m-m-m-m-m-m-m-m-m-m-m-m-m-m-m!"

Then one day a tall, thin man walked into the store.

He had very big feet!

"Clump, Clump, Clump!
Swish, Squash, Clump!"
screeched his shoes.

He walked right over to me and

took me off the shelf.

"Yip-p-e-e-e-e-e-e-e-e-e-e-e-e-e!" I screamed. "Maybe, this will be my lucky day to see the world."

Then the tall man sat down and removed his smelly, old shoes from his big, stinky feet.

"Phew-oo-oo-oo-wee!" I exclaimed.

"What was that horrible smell?" But he ignored me and pushed me onto his big, stinky feet!

His feet smelled like toilets with rotten eggs falling out of them.

I smelled like rotten eggs, too.

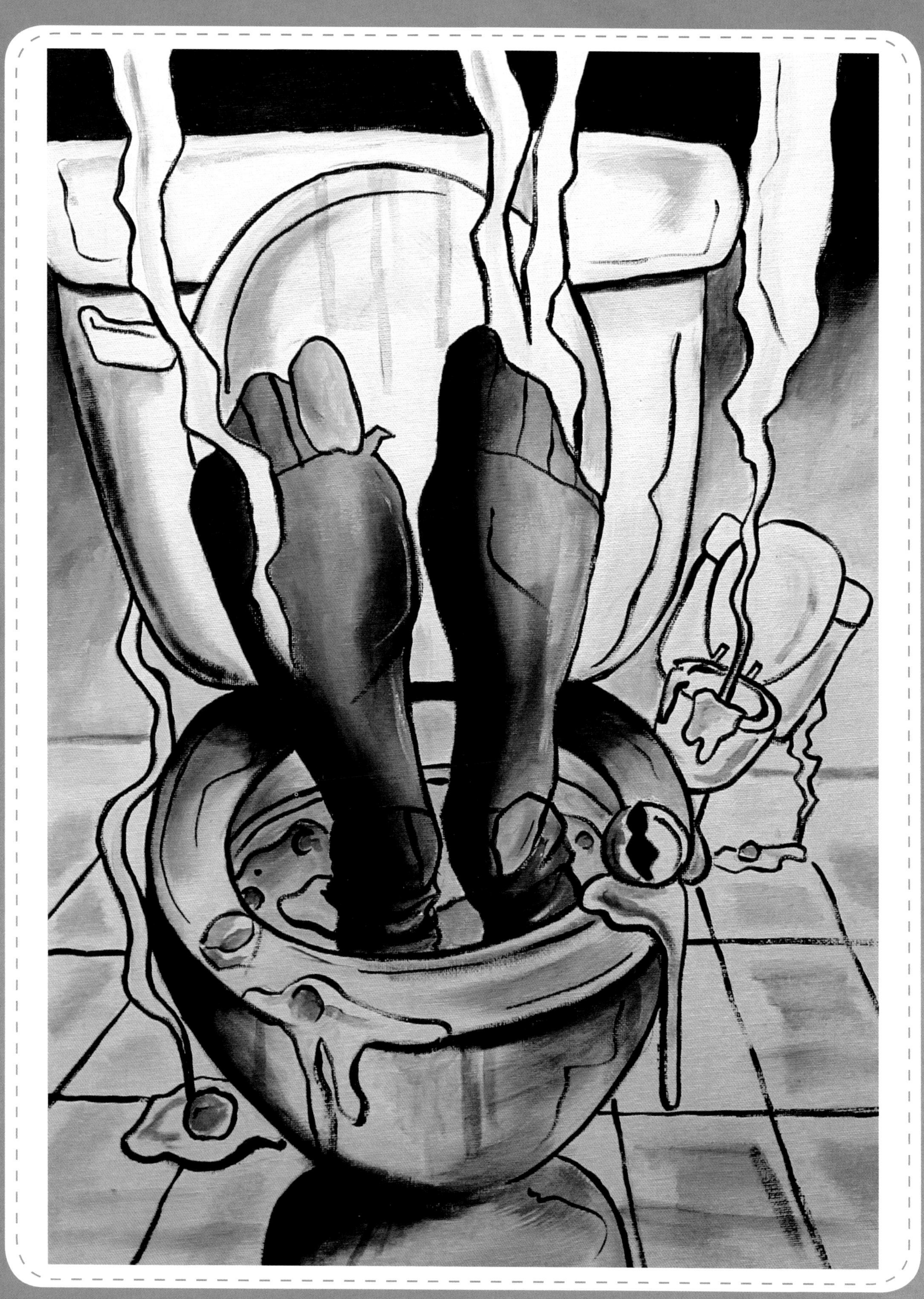

The tall, thin man with the big, stinky feet walked around the store for a minute....

Clump! Clump! Clump! ....
Swish, Squash, Clump!

He paid the cashier and left the store with his stinky feet leaving a **strong** *odor behind him....*

Phew-oo-oo-oo-wee!

The tall, thin man with big, stinky feet walked all around town all day long until nightfall.

He fell into a swamp that sneezed green, slimy frogs all over me.

Phew-oo-oo-oo-wee!

As the night grew darker, he stumbled along, because he was so-o-o-o-o-o tired and sleepy.

Finally, he saw a long bench in a park, sat down to rest, and fell fast asleep.

Z-z-z-z-z-z-z-z-z-z-z-z-z-z-
z-z-z-z-z-z-z-z-z-z-z-z-z-z-
z-z-z-z-Snort, Snort, Snort,
z-z-z-z-z-z-z-z-z-z-z.

"Yip-p-e-e-e-e-e-e-e-
e-e-e-e-e-e!"

This was my big chance to wiggle away from these stinky feet and never smell stinky again.

So I pushed and I pulled. I kicked and I screamed. At first, nothing worked.

I screamed,

"H-e-l-p me-e-e-e!"

Then suddenly, I saw lightning flash across the sky, and I heard thunder clashing like cymbals and then humming like a drum roll through the night.

It started raining....

At first, it was a sprinkle. Gradually, it became a cascade of water drenching me.

I kicked and kicked, but I was stuck to his feet like glue hanging on for dear life.

The flood of water grew larger and larger *until the sky poured buckets of rain over me.*
It was slippery and extremely wet. So I kicked harder ...

and **harder**... *and*

harder... *and*

harder... *until I flew into the stormy sky.*

"Ah-h-h-h-h-h-h-h-h-h-h-h," I sighed.

I could breathe again.

I flew higher and higher into the very, wet sky and grew cleaner and cleaner as the rain washed the stink away. This was heavenly!

Of course, whatever goes up

must

come

down!

So I fell down, ...

down, ...

down, ...

and hoped for a smooth landing.

I was clean and not smelly

anymore.

But **... ... ...** *OH, NO!*

Where was I falling?

This couldn't be happening to me.

I fell into something even
stinkier than the tall man's
big, stinky feet.

I fell into ...

a garbage can!

"Phew-oo-oo-oo-wee!"

It was smell-l-l-l-l-l-ly."

It made me stinky all over again.

"Oh, no."

I was suffocating and gasping for fresh air again. So I started kicking and kicking harder and harder and harder and

harder ...

until ... finally, ... I flew into the sky again.

"Ah-h-h-h-h-h-h-h-h-h-h-h-h-h-h-h-h-h-h-h."

The rain washed me clean again.

As you know, whatever goes up...

must come down.

So I began falling down, ...

down, ...

down, ...

down, ...

lower,

and lower,

and lower,

until ...

I floated gently onto a bed of fresh, green grass.

I could breathe again.

"Ah-h-h-h-h-h-h-h!"

That was exhausting!

That was tiring.

Now I am clean, clean,
clean again, and not
stinky, stinky, stinky
again.
I can rest now.

H-h-h-h-m-m-m-m-m-m-m-

m-m-m-m-m-m-m-m-m-m-

m-m-m-m-m-m-m-m-m-m-

m-m-m-m-m-m-m-m-m-m-

m-m-m-m-m-m-m-m-m-m-

m-m-m-m-m-m-m-m-m-m-

....

Can you help me find my way back to the shoe store?

The End

Critical Thinking
Learning Activities

The Critical Thinking Activities are designed for students in grades Kindergarten -2nd grade as well as for struggling readers in grades 3-5 to provide rigor and enrichment for gifted, primary grade students and to provide scaffolding for struggling readers in the intermediate grades.

1. *What is the moral of the story, Stinky Shoes? Explain.*
2. *Design a timeline for the Stinky Shoes.*
3. *Write a biography for the Stinky Shoes.*
4. *Discover and analyze the use of adjectives, similes, metaphors, alliteration, personification, palindromes, and onomatopoeia in the story.*
5. *Describe how the shoes looked and smelled after they had fallen into the stinky places. Add words to develop oxymorons:*
   i.e. The shoes smelled like fresh, rotten eggs in the garbage can.
6. *Explain how adjectives, similes, metaphors, alliteration, personification, palindromes, oxymorons, hyperboles, and/or onomatopoeia are used to animate the story.*
7. *Create a new ending for the story, Stinky Shoes.*
8. *Write a sequel to the story, Stinky Shoes.*
9. *Design a sign or a poster to promote the book, Stinky Shoes.*
10. *Would you categorize this book, Stinky Shoes, as juvenile fiction, language arts, or another category and why?*

About the Author

Debra J. Mines grew up in Cleveland, Ohio. After graduation from high school, she attended Ohio Wesleyan University and graduated with a Bachelor of Arts Degree in Elementary Education with a concentration in Reading instruction. Soon after graduation, she married the late Herman C. Mines and enjoyed family life with him and their two children, whom they read to continuously.

During these years Debra J. Mines also graduated from Case Western Reserve University with a Master of Arts Degree in Curriculum and Instruction with specialization in Reading Supervision and completed all but the dissertation for a doctorate in Educational Administration from the University of Akron.

Debra J. Mines' teaching career began in the East Cleveland City Schools and later continued in the Fulton County Schools and the DeKalb County School District in Georgia. She has taught children to read and write from Kindergarten through ninth grade. Additional highlights of her career include teaching graduate-level courses as a part-time instructor at Cleveland State University, teaching graduate courses for the Summer Institute for Reading Intervention sponsored by Ohio's Northeast Regional Professional Development Center, and attaining certification as a National Board Certified Teacher.

Finally, as a professional teacher and life-long learner, she is compelled to learn as much as possible about her students, their cultures and communities. This desire motivated her to complete programs for the English Speakers of Other Languages (ESOL) Endorsement and the Gifted In-Field Endorsement. She enjoys teaching diverse populations of students and looks forward to continuing to share her stories, knowledge, and skills to help each child to reach his/her highest potential.

About the Illustrator

Henry M. Blackmon III grew up in Decatur, Georgia, a suburb of Atlanta where he currently lives and works as a middle school art instructor. His passion for art began at the age of three where he was surrounded by his father's classic jazz music and his mother's classical and show tune music. The visual arts were also represented in the home through various publications including the cover art of Norman Rockwell from the Saturday Evening Post as well as vintage Coca Cola art and the comic book art of Jack Kirby which captured Henry's imagination.

Henry proclaimed to his kindergarten teacher that he would one day draw children's books. Blackmon won his first art competition by drawing the cover of his favorite book, Treasure Island, by Robert Louis Stevenson in 1980 when he was in 2nd grade. Henry continued to excel in art throughout school beating out high school juniors and seniors as an 8th grader in the annual Black History Art contest in 1986 and winning the DeKalb County Schools and National Task Force Against Drug Abuse poster contest in 1987.

In the Fall of 1990, Henry took his skills to his father's alma mater, Morris Brown College, in Atlanta, Georgia to pursue his degree in Fine Arts with a concentration in illustration. He continued to excel being named Mr. Fine Arts for homecoming 1992 and graduated with the highest average of all fine art majors in 1994. While working on portfolios and completing applications for illustration firms including Disney, Henry was asked to step in as the art teacher at a local summer camp. This experience was life changing for him. He realized how desperately inner city kids needed a male role model such as himself and felt he could make a difference. Henry decided to go back to school adding on an art education certificate from Georgia State University. Henry Blackmon has been in education for twenty-three years teaching in both DeKalb and Atlanta Public Schools and is currently teaching middle school art in Atlanta.

Henry has still maintained a strong presence in the visual arts displaying his art around the southeast including The National Black Arts Festival, The Tubman Museum, The Georgia State Capitol, Alabama State University, Fayetteville State University, Art Station and a host of other venues. Blackmon is known as the narrative artist due to the storytelling nature of several of his current pieces.

Today, Blackmon's work is personified by bold colors with the use of mostly watercolor and acrylic. Henry is constantly experimenting with different ways of storytelling through art and especially excited to pursue this adventure through his first children's book, Stinky Shoes.

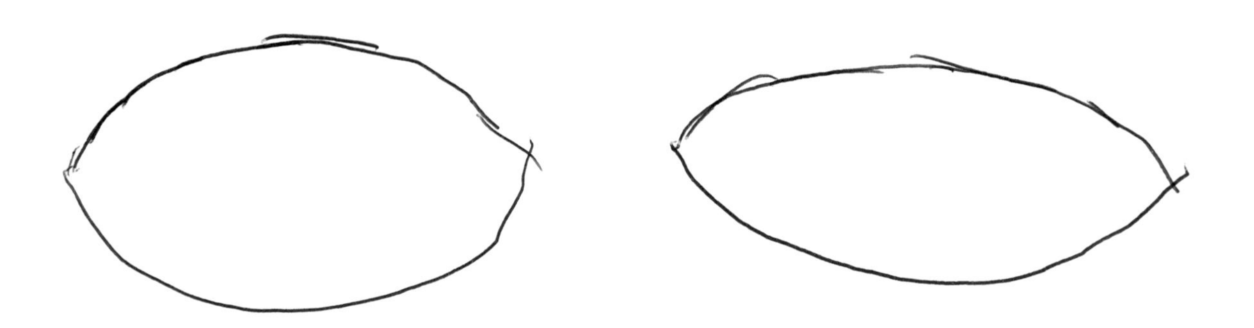